The Beyond Beautiful Treasure Box

Protecting Your Inner Treasures

Written by: Julia Grace Saffold

Inspired by: Jasmine Y. Zapata, MD, MPH

Illustrated by: Jonah Anderson

ISBN-13: 978-0-692-97081-2

"Just as a single snowflake falls from the sky, uniquely different than all the rest, so each of us is divinely fashioned to be beyond beautiful in our own special way."

Julia Saffold a.k.a. "Mama Jewels"

DEDICATION

I dedicate this book to my adorable grandchildren, Miguel (MJ) and Aameira. You are the light of my world, and Nana hopes that you will embrace every valuable lesson that is explored in this book. To my soon-to-be born grandchild, Lillyana Gracelia, and to my future generations, you are riding in on a powerful legacy of love. Your great grandfather, Rev. Dr. Sandy Johnson stated a motto for our family which is to "spread love, inspire hope, and to ignite change." May you walk in this powerful legacy all the days of your life. With all my heart....

Love, Nana

BEYOND BEAUTIFUL DECLARATION

By: Jasmine Zapata, MD, MPH

Today will be a great day!
I'll achieve all I set my mind to.
I cannot be stopped!
I can do anything I want to.

Cuz I'm beyond beautiful. I'm BEYOND Beautiful!

I'm courageous
I'm resilient
I'm confident
I'm creative

I am talented, intelligent, unique and innovative!

I'm worth it. I deserve it.
I am treasured. I am loved.

I deserve every blessing that is coming from above!

FOREWORD

Thank you for taking the time to read this book. Now more than ever, we must empower and inspire our young people. The Beyond Beautiful Declaration was written to inspire youth around the world, that in addition to their outer appearances, what matters most is what is on the INSIDE.

Each child possesses hidden treasures within, like courage, resilience, confidence, creativity, talent, intelligence and so much more! These are very important qualities needed to succeed in life and one must never let anyone else take them away! As a pediatrician and preventive health doctor, I have seen first-hand how important these qualities are for the mental and physical health of children! As you read this book, think about how each character resonates with you. Think about similar situations you have encountered in your life. Think about ways you can use the things you have gone through to inspire, empower, and encourage the next generation!

I'm SO extremely thankful that my mother, Julia Grace Saffold, worked hard to instill these values inside of me and I am now working toward instilling these same values into the next generation. Now more than ever, it's time to pour into our young people, like never before!

This book is an amazing tool!! Time to reclaim those treasures!

Jasmine Zapata, MD, MPH
www.DrJasmineZapata.com

INTRODUCTION

This is a book about embracing the beautiful treasures that we possess inside, as well as the beauty that lies in others. It is about learning how to cultivate healthy self-esteem, yet remaining humble enough to help and build others up. It is about learning to see through the lenses of people who may be different than us, while growing in our capacity to understand the strengths, values, and needs of those we interact with. There are many golden nuggets hidden between the lines of this fairytale. My hope is that parents, grandparents, aunts, uncles, big sisters, big brothers, teachers, mentors, counselors, youth leaders, etc. will take the time to engage in those conversations that both challenge as well as build up the younger generation and the generations to come.

-Julia Saffold a.k.a. "Mama Jewels"

CONTENTS

CHAPTER 1

A VERY SPECIAL BOX

Once upon a time in a land far away, there lived a beautiful little girl named Princess Aameira. She, along with her dashing, slightly older brother, Prince Miguel, lived in a wonderful land called, Beyond Beautiful.

Beyond Beautiful was an amazing place to live. It was filled with trees, flowers, green grass, lakes, ponds, swings, swimming pools, and lots of playgrounds.

There were ducks, birds, butterflies, squirrels, dogs, cats, fish, and all kinds of beautiful things in nature for them to enjoy.

When Princess Aameira and Prince Miguel were born, they were given a very special gift. It was a beautiful golden treasure box.

But, this was no ordinary treasure box, because this treasure box was filled with all kinds of shiny gems and jewels that gave Princess Aameira and Prince Miguel very special abilities.

CHAPTER 2

SHIMMERING JEWELS

COURAGE, CONFIDENCE, TALENT, CREATIVITY

Each day, Princess Aameira would take the shiny jewels out of her treasure box and, one by one, hold them close to her heart. She would dance and sing, "Today will be a great day. I'll achieve all I set my mind to. I cannot be stopped. I can do anything I want to, because I'm Beyond Beautiful!"

One of her favorite jewels was called COURAGE.

Courage was a shiny beautiful gemstone that helped her to never be afraid of doing the right thing, no matter how hard it was.

Another glimmering jewel was called CONFIDENCE.

Confidence gave the princess special abilities to believe that she could do or be anything she set her mind to, if she just worked hard enough.

There were so many other amazing treasures in her box, like TALENT and CREATIVITY. These helped her create and do the most amazing things you could ever imagine.

CHAPTER 3

GLOWING TREASURES

INNOVATION INTELLIGENCE, RESILIENCE, SELF-WORTH

In the very middle of Princess Aameira's treasure box were two smooth, round, and very shiny gems. They had a beautiful glow whenever you looked at them.

One of them was called INNOVATION and the other was called INTELLIGENCE.

Innovation always helped Princess Aameira think of brand new ideas that no one else ever thought of before. Intelligence made her very smart and helped her to get excellent grades in school.

Finally, way at the bottom of her box, there were two gigantic treasures that glittered and shimmered with gold. They were so big and so shiny, that they lit up the entire box.

One of them was called RESILIENCE and the other one was called SELF-WORTH.

Resilience helped her to never give up and always try again, even when things didn't go well the first time. Self-worth taught her how to love herself for who she was, and not for what other people thought or said about her.

CHAPTER 4

THE UGLY FROG QUEEN

One day, when Princess Aameira was walking in the flower gardens, along came the ugly frog Queen, who said to the princess, "Hello beautiful Princess Aameira. You are the smartest, most talented, and courageous girl in the land. I have a little favor to ask of you. Can you help me?"

But Princess Aameira wondered, "What could the Ugly Frog Queen want with me?"

She knew the frog queen was usually up to no good. So, the princess said to the frog queen, "What is the problem you are having Ms. Frog Queen?"

The ugly queen answered, "You see, I have a friend who is in trouble, because she's lost all of her COURAGE and CONFIDENCE.

She's afraid, and no longer believes in herself. Oh Princess, could I please borrow your Courage and Confidence, just for one day, so that my friend can be helped?"

But Princess Aameira quickly answered, "Oh, no, Ms. Frog Queen, I cannot give away my treasures to anyone or I may lose them."

But the ugly frog Queen said to the princess, "If you let me borrow your treasures, I promise I will bring them back to you tomorrow."

Princess Aameira thought about it really hard, and reluctantly said, "Ok, you may borrow my Courage and Confidence, but only for a day. You have to promise to return them to me tomorrow."

The frog queen replied, "Yes, little princess, I will. I promise."

"Being Beyond Beautiful is about being patient with ourselves and with others."

Julia Saffold a.k.a. "Mama Jewels"

CHAPTER 5

TREASURES LOST

When the next day came, the princess rushed back to the garden to meet the frog queen, and when she arrived, the frog queen said, "Oh Princess Aameira, I'm so sorry but my friend not only lost her Confidence and her Courage, but now has lost her TALENT and CREATIVITY too." She can no longer imagine or create anything. If only you would let me borrow your Talent and

Creativity just for one day. I promise I will return them all to you, this same time tomorrow."

But when tomorrow came, the princess was tricked again by the ugly frog queen. Each day the Princess met the frog queen hoping to get her treasures back, but she was tricked into giving more of her treasures away each day.

Princess Aameira began to feel ugly, weak, and afraid. She no longer felt the courage she needed to resist the queen's powers.

Princess Aameira began to doubt who she was, forgetting all the wonderful ideas she once had. She ended up giving all her treasures away to the ugly frog queen.

CHAPTER 6

PRINCE MIGUEL HELPS

Prince Miguel noticed one day, that the Princess looked very sad. He asked, "Sister, sister, what's wrong? Why are you sad, and why do you look so afraid?"

She answered and said, "Oh, brother, I've lost my confidence and courage and all of my other treasures. I have given them all away to the Ugly Frog Queen." Prince Miguel said, "Why did you give your treasures away? You were supposed to guard them and protect them with all your heart."

"I know, I know", said the princess sadly. "The ugly queen tricked me by saying she'd give them back to me, but she didn't", she explained.

Prince Miguel was very angry and said, "That ugly frog queen is very sneaky and tricky too. She had no right to take your treasures. We must go at once, to see Mr. Wise Old Owl. He can tell us how to get your treasures back."

"Oh yes", the princess declared, "Mr. Wise Old Owl will tell us what to do! He's very smart and he knows a lot of things".

CHAPTER 7

THE WISE OLD OWL

So, Prince Miguel took his sister by the hand, and together they went to find Mr. Wise Old Owl to ask for his help.

When the wise old owl heard about what the ugly frog queen had done, he told them that there was only one way they could recover Princess Aameira's treasures.

He said to her, "My dear princess, you must first learn the powerful secret that makes all your treasures work if you want to get them back from the ugly frog queen."

"The secret? What powerful secret?" asked Prince Miguel and Princess Aameira. "You must use the Secret Key", said the wise old owl. Prince Miguel. exclaimed, "What key do you speak of Mr. Owl?"

So, the wise old owl grabbed a book off of the shelf and began to teach them all about their inner treasures. He taught them all about love and self-worth. He taught them how to keep a strong mind. He read to them all about beauty and strength that comes from the inside.

Finally, he taught them all about resilience and how to bounce back from their mistakes.

"Being Beyond Beautiful is about striving to be the best "me" that I can be. It's about going forward and not looking back."

Julia Saffold a.k.a. "Mama Jewels"

CHAPTER 8

THE SECRET KEY

Princess Aameira asked the wise old owl again.

"Sir, what exactly is this special key I need to use?"

The old owl turned and looked her straight into her eyes. "My dear princess, you were born with each of the gifts that are found in your treasure box. These gifts are already inside of you.

29

Always remember that only YOU, hold the key to protect your inner treasures from being stolen."

"But they were stolen Mr. Owl. Please tell me how I can get them back?"

"The KEY, my dear princess, is that you have to BELIEVE with all of your heart that the treasures belong to you", said Mr. Owl.

"Is that all she has to do?" asked Prince Miguel.

"Yes" said the wise old owl. "If you can believe, I mean really believe, then you hold the key that will break the power of the ugly frog queen and get your treasures back."

"Now look deep within your heart Princess Aameira. Do you believe that the treasures are yours?" asked the wise old owl.

At first, princess Aameira wasn't sure because she had lost so much. But Prince Miguel said, "Sister, I will stand with you. I believe in you. You are beautiful and courageous. You are resilient and creative. You can be anything you want to be. You can achieve anything you set your mind to. You just have to believe!"

"Beyond beautiful is about building up and not tearing down."

Julia Saffold a.k.a. "Mama Jewels"

CHAPTER 9

TREASURES RECOVERED

Princess Aameira began to feel her strength returning. "Yes, I believe" she shouted. "The treasures are mine and I want them back!"

So, the prince and princess left at once to go find the ugly frog queen and demand she give back the treasures.

They found the ugly frog queen sitting on an old stump down by the river swamp. She was looking through all of the treasures, trying to figure out how to make them work.

The prince and princess walked up to the frog queen and demanded, "You ugly frog queen, we're here to take the princesses' treasures back!"

But the Ugly Frog Queen just laughed and said "Ha, Ha, Ha, I will not give them back. They are mine now, and soon I will be just as beautiful, talented, creative, intelligent, courageous, and resilient as Princess Aameira."

But, just then, Princess Aameira remembered all the words that the wise old owl had told her.

34

She remembered that the key to breaking the ugly frog queen's power was that she had to believe with all her heart that the treasures belonged to her.

So Princess Aameira took a deep breath, and with all the strength she could muster up, proclaimed,

"You are a thief and a robber, ugly frog queen! I hold the key to the treasures in my heart. You only have the power to take them away from me if I let you. I may have made the mistake of letting you trick me into giving away my treasures, but I'm strong and resilient and I demand that you give them all back to me! I'm courageous! I'm resilient! I'm confident! I'm creative! I'm talented! I'm intelligent! I'm unique and innovative! I am worth it! I deserve it! I am treasured! I am loved! I deserve every blessing that is coming from above!"

Prince Miguel came and stood by his sister, and repeated with her, over and over, "We're courageous! We're resilient! We're confident! We're creative!

We're talented! We're intelligent! We're unique and Innovative!

We are worth it! We deserve it! We are treasured! We are loved! We deserve every blessing that is coming from above!"

Each time they declared it, the frog queen became weaker, until she finally gave up, and returned the princesses' Treasure Box.

"Oh, Princess Aameira," said the ugly frog queen. "I just wanted to be like you."

"I thought if I could just have your treasures, I wouldn't feel so lonely, sad and ugly anymore. I wish to be happy, and love myself. I wish to become as beautiful as you."

Princess Aameira's heart suddenly melted for the frog queen, and she softly answered, "Oh, Ms. Frog Queen, I never knew you felt that way, and I deeply apologize for calling you ugly so many times."

"I have learned a valuable lesson today, that everyone deserves to be loved, even you. Real beauty can't be measured by what's on the outside, but real beauty comes from inside our hearts. Learning to love and respect ourselves and others, is what truly makes us Beyond Beautiful."

"Ms. beautiful frog queen, if you look deep within your heart, you too will find your very own treasure box, filled with wonderful qualities that make you uniquely you," said the Princess.

"But you must start by believing in yourself. You are worth it. You deserve it. You are treasured, and you are loved. You deserve every blessing that is coming from above."

"You never have to steal treasures from others to feel good about yourself, because we all have a treasure box full of inner strengths and qualities that make us uniquely beautiful in our own way."

"We all make mistakes, Ms. Frog Queen, but you must love yourself enough to believe that YOU are not a mistake, and that we can always try again by making better choices."

Prince Miguel felt the same way as Princess Aameira, and apologized to the frog queen saying, "We're sorry to hear that you have been feeling so sad and alone. We thought that you were just a mean old frog who wanted people to leave you alone. But, now we see that you want to have friends too."

"Even though it was my sister who lost her treasures, I learned a valuable lesson too. I learned that we all need someone to care about us and that includes you Ms. Frog Queen. We shouldn't have called you all those mean things."

"Would you like to come to the playground with us tomorrow for some fun and games?"

The frog queen happily replied, "Oh yes, yes, yes, I would love to, and thank you so very much for inviting me. I've never had friends before".

"Thanks to you both, I choose to believe in myself that I too am Beyond Beautiful in my own special way. Never again will I steal from others, but will work to be the 'best me' that I can be."

From that day on, the prince, the princess, and the frog queen became best friends and helped many others to unlock the unlimited potential of their own Beyond Beautiful Treasures.

The End

"Being Beyond Beautiful is about our capacity to LOVE. To love not only ourselves, but also our fellow man. Being beyond beautiful goes so much deeper than surface level appearances, popularity, makeup, clothing, or socioeconomic status. Learning to love ourselves and others is a life long journey of self-reflection, empathy, acceptance, and yes, forgiveness."

Julia Saffold a.k.a. "Mama Jewels"

CHAPTER 10

REFLECTION QUESTIONS

THE FOLLOWING QUESTIONS CAN BE USED AS DISCUSSION STARTERS TO PROMOTE HEALTHY COMMUNICATION, ACUTE AWARENESS AND POSITIVE CHANGE. MY PRAYER IS THAT WE INCREASE OUR CAPACITY TO LOVE AS WE CELEBRATE ALL THE BEYOND BEAUTIFUL TREASURES THAT LIE WITHIN.

1) OUT OF ALL THE TREASURES IN PRINCESS AAMEIRA'S TREASURE BOX, WHICH ONE WAS YOUR FAVORITE? WHY?

2) WHAT IS YOUR DEFINITION OF "BEYOND BEAUTIFUL?" WHAT IS ONE OF THE MOST IMPORTANT TREASURES YOU HAVE INSIDE OF YOU?

3) HAS SOMEONE OR SOMETHING EVER TRIED TO STEAL ONE OF YOUR INNER TREASURES? IF SO, HOW DID YOU GET IT BACK?

4) WHAT WAS THE WISE OLD OWL'S ADVICE TO PRINCESS AAMEIRA?

5) WHAT IS THE "SECRET KEY" AND HOW CAN YOU USE IT IN YOUR OWN LIFE?

6) CAN YOU RELATE WITH ANY OF THE CHARACTERS IN THE BOOK? IN WHAT WAYS?

7) WHY DO YOU THINK SOME PEOPLE GIVE AWAY THEIR INNER TREASURES? WHAT ADVICE WOULD YOU GIVE THEM?

8) DO YOU THINK IT WAS HARD FOR PRINCESS AAMEIRA AND PRINCE MIGUEL TO FORGIVE THE UGLY FROG QUEEN? WHY OR WHY NOT?

9) WHY DO YOU THINK IT IS SO IMPORTANT TO PROTECT YOUR INNER TREASURES?

10) WHAT SPECIFIC THINGS CAN YOU DO TO PROTECT YOUR INNER TREASURES?

SPECIAL ACKNOWLEDGEMENTS

I would, first, like to thank my Heavenly Father for His unconditional love and provision, all the days of my life. I also wish to honor the memory of my parents, Sandy and Roylene Johnson, whose love and support for me, throughout my entire life, has provided me with the solid foundation of faith, love and family, on which I stand today.

To my husband, Mel, who has been my rock through good, bad, happy, sad, in sickness, and in health -- I thank you dear, for your undying love and support for me in all my pursuits.

To my amazing daughter, Jasmine Yvonne, who is my heart — I am honored to acknowledge you for the joy and life-giving inspiration you have been to me. It's funny how the roles have flipped. I raised you up from a child, and watched you blossom into a beautiful mother, wife, doctor, author, youth empowerment coach, and leader. You leaned on me for a season. But, when the seasons shifted, you took care of me, and helped me through some of the toughest days of my life. It is an honor to be your mother and to watch you live your dreams. It is your passion, drive, courage, and determination, that has inspired me to write this book. Thank you for, not only your love for me, but also for putting me through your book writing coaching course, which has now resulted in my first published book. This monumental mother-daughter joint book release, will go down in history as one of the best things that has ever happened to me. You are an amazing daughter, my beyond beautiful, sweet angel. I love you and I thank you.

Finally, a special thank you to Jonah Anderson for the amazing artwork done for this book; to Greg Doby, for the beautiful cover design; to Sister Catrina Sparkman, for planting the first seed in me to become a writer: to my loving sister, Jennifer for your creative & contagious love for our family; to my brother, Jon, for your stable love and support; and to everyone else who has ever believed in me and supported me on my journey. I THANK YOU ALL.

Love, Julie

ABOUT THE ILLUSTRATOR

My name is Jonah Anderson. I am 17 and a young artist born in Milwaukee, but raised in Madison, Wisconsin. Inspired by comic books, I've always enjoyed drawing characters. Drawing and creating is an everyday thing for me and with practice I've gained valuable experience in the visual arts. My skills have continuously grown with time. I enjoy exploring my passion whenever possible. I create my own short stories and illustrations, t-shirt designs, and I've also entered and won contests using my artistic gifts.

Jonah Anderson, Illustrator
jpanderson2k@gmail.com

ABOUT THE AUTHOR

Julia Grace Saffold is a native of Milwaukee WI, currently residing in Madison, WI. She is a devoted wife, mother, and grandmother whose passion in life is to inspire individuals to reach their highest potential. She is an author, evangelist, choral director, youth empowerment coach, and team builder. Inspired by the life work of her daughter, pediatrician, Jasmine Zapata, MD, MPH, Julia loves inspiring the younger generation to embrace keys that unlock their inner treasures, and lead to unlimited potential in their lives.

In a joint mother-daughter collaboration, Julia's newest release, "The Beyond Beautiful Treasure Box – Protecting Your Inner Treasures", along with her daughter's newest release, "Beyond Beautiful – A Girl's Guide to Unlocking the Power of Inner Beauty, Self Esteem, Resilience and Courage" provides powerful tools to unlock unlimited potential in the lives of young people all over the world.

To stay connected with Julia, please visit www.NewSeasonShift.com

www.ingramcontent.com/pod-product-compliance
Lightning Source LLC
Chambersburg PA
CBHW041729240626
47171CB00001B/5